# ANANSI THE SPIDER

a tale from the Ashanti

adapted and
illustrated by
Gerald McDermott

Holt, Rinehart and Winston
New York

A HOLT REINFORCED EDITION

"ANANSI THE SPIDER is adapted from an animated
film by Gerald McDermott produced by
LANDMARK PRODUCTION INCORPORATED"

Published by Holt, Rinehart and Winston,
383 Madison Avenue, New York, New York, 10017.
Published simultaneously in Canada by Holt, Rinehart
and Winston of Canada, Limited.

Library of Congress Catalog Number: 76-150028

ISBN: 0-03-088368-7

Printed in the United States of America

15   14   13   12   11   10   9

ISBN 0-03-088368-7

Ghana

for my
Mother
and
Father

First son was called See Trouble. He had the gift of seeing trouble a long way off.

Second son was Road Builder.

Thirsty son was River Drinker.

Next son
was
Game Skinner.

Another son
was
Stone Thrower.

And last of sons
was Cushion.
He was
very soft.

All were
good sons
of Anansi.

One time Anansi
went a long way
from home.

Far from home.

He got lost.                    He fell into trouble.

Back home was son See Trouble
"Father is in danger!" he cried.
He knew it quickly
and he told those other sons.

Road Builder son
said, "Follow me!"

Off he went,
making a road.

They went fast,
those six brothers,
gone to help Anansi.

"Where is
father now?"

"Fish has
swallowed him!"
"Anansi is
inside Fish."

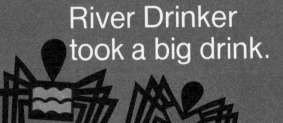

River Drinker
took a big drink.

No more river.

Then Game Skinner
helped father Anansi.
He split open Fish.

More trouble came,
right then.

It was Falcon
took Anansi
up in the Sky.

"Quick now
Stone Thrower!"

The stone hit Falcon.
Anansi fell
through the sky.

Now Cushion ran
to help father.

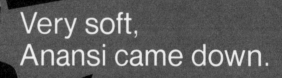

Very soft,
Anansi came down.

They were very happy
that spider family.

All home again
that night,
Kwaku Anansi found
a thing in the forest.

"What is this?
A great globe of light?"

"O mysterious and beautiful!
I shall give this to my son,"
said Anansi,
"To the son who rescued me!"

"But which son of six …
Which deserves the prize?"

"Nyame, can you help me? O Nyame!" called Anansi.

For Ashanti people,
Nyame is The God of All Things.

Anansi
asked this
of Nyame—
"Please hold
the beautiful
globe of light
until I know
which son
should have it
for his own."

And so they tried
to decide which son
deserved the prize.
They tried,
but they
could not decide.
They argued
all night.

Nyame saw this.

The God of All Things,
He took
the beautiful white light
up into the sky.

He keeps it there
for all to see.
It is still there.
It will always be there.

It is there tonight.

## ABOUT THE AUTHOR

Gerald McDermott was born in Detroit, Michigan, and now lives with his wife, an artist, in the south of France. Though primarily a film-maker, Mr. McDermott is fascinated with the art of book illustration. Of this, his first venture into the book form, Mr. McDermott writes: "Anansi required unique development, to fit his unique qualities. The search for compelling character and design demanded innovation. Throughout, I went to the graphics of the Ashanti people for my direction, to their simple but sophisticated combinations of geometric forms, to their limited color schemes, to their stylized animals and plants." The film version of ANANSI THE SPIDER won the 1970 Blue Ribbon at the American Film Festival; *Wilson Library Bulletin* called it one of "the two most popular children's films produced in 1970."

## ABOUT THE BOOK

ANANSI THE SPIDER artwork is preseparated in four colors. The type is Helvetica. The book is printed by offset.